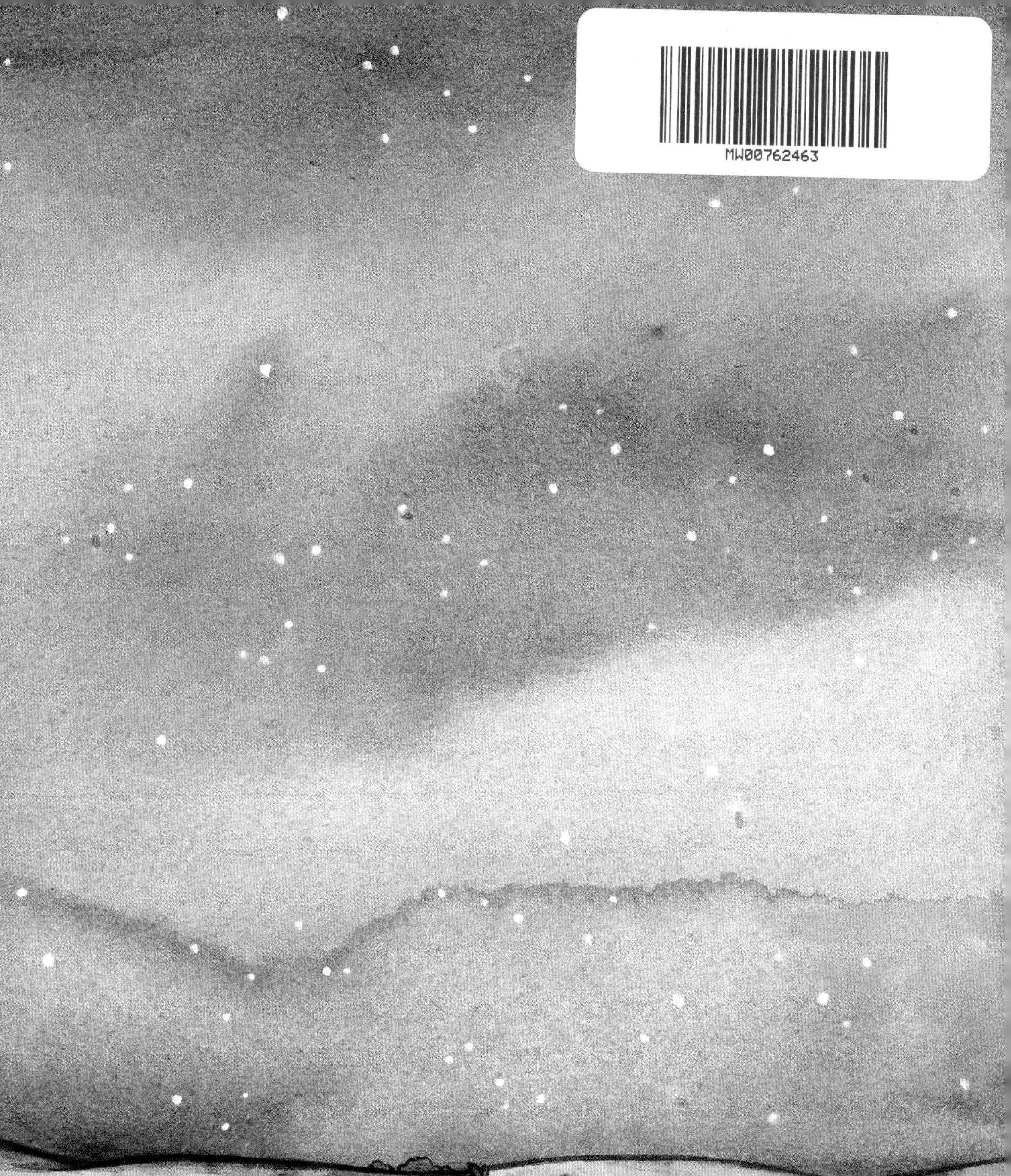

The Gifts They Gave

Patricia Reeder Eubank

STERLING CHILDREN'S BOOKS
New York

An Imprint of Sterling Publishing
387 Park Avenue South
New York, NY 10016

STERLING CHILDREN'S BOOKS and the distinctive Sterling Children's Books logo
are trademarks of Sterling Publishing Co., Inc.

Design by Jennifer Browning

ISBN 978-1-4549-0508-0

Distributed in Canada by Sterling Publishing
c/o Canadian Manda Group, 165 Dufferin Street
Toronto, Ontario, Canada M6K 3H6
Distributed in the United Kingdom by GMC Distribution Services
Castle Place, 166 High Street, Lewes, East Sussex, England BN7 1XU
Distributed in Australia by Capricorn Link (Australia) Pty. Ltd.
P.O. Box 704, Windsor, NSW 2756, Australia

For information about custom editions, special sales, and premium and corporate purchases, please contact Sterling Special Sales at 800-805-5489 or specialsales@sterlingpublishing.com.

Manufactured in China
Lot #:
4 6 8 10 9 7 5
07/16

www.sterlingpublishing.com/kids

For Carlyle, who is such a beautiful, insightful, creative writer, an amazing runner, an artistic craftsman of furniture, who greatly loves dogs and the outdoors, who does everything with such depth of thought, discipline, and determination, and who has such a caring heart that is always willing to help someone.

Jesus, our brother, kind and good,
was humbly born in a stable of wood.
And the friendly beasts around him stood.
Jesus, our brother, kind and good.

“I,” said the donkey, shaggy and brown,
“I carried his mother uphill and down.
I carried her safely to Bethlehem town.
I,” said the donkey, shaggy and brown.

"I," said the cow, all white and red,
"I gave him my manger for his bed.
I gave him my hay to pillow his head.
I," said the cow, all white and red.

"I," said the sheep with the curly horn,
"I gave him my wool for a blanket warm.
He wore my coat on Christmas morn.
I," said the sheep with the curly horn.

"I," said the camel, yellow and black,
"over the desert upon my back,
I brought him gifts in the wise man's pack.
I," said the camel, yellow and black.

"I," said the barn cat, calico bright,
"watched Mary's joy that most holy night.
Purred a lullaby while she held him tight.
I," said the barn cat, calico bright.

"I," said the shepherd's dog, black and white,
"guarded our King 'neath the star's shining light.
Wagged my tail to welcome him right.
I," said the shepherd's dog, black and white.

"I," said the dove from the rafters high,
"I cooed him to sleep so he would not cry.
We cooed him to sleep, my mate and I.
I," said the dove from the rafters high.

Thus every beast by some good spell,
in the stable dark was glad to tell,
of the gift he gave Emmanuel,
the gift he gave Emmanuel.

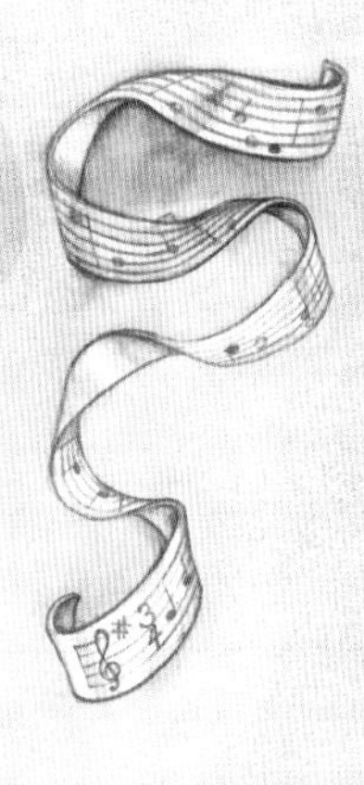

Jesus, our brother, kind and good,
was humbly born in a stable of wood.
And the friendly beasts around him stood.
Jesus, our brother, kind and good.

"I," said the donkey, shaggy and brown,
"I carried his mother uphill and down.
I carried her safely to Bethlehem town.
I," said the donkey, shaggy and brown.

"I," said the cow, all white and red,
"I gave him my manger for his bed.
I gave him my hay to pillow his head.
I," said the cow, all white and red.

"I," said the sheep with the curly horn,
"I gave him my wool for a blanket warm.
He wore my coat on Christmas morn.
I," said the sheep with the curly horn.

"I," said the camel, yellow and black,
"over the desert upon my back,
I brought him gifts in the wise man's pack.
I," said the camel, yellow and black.

"I," said the barn cat, calico bright,
"watched Mary's joy that most holy night.
Purred a lullaby while she held him tight.
I," said the barn cat, calico bright.

"I," said the shepherd's dog, black and white,
"guarded our King 'neath the star's shining light.
Wagged my tail to welcome him right.
I," said the shepherd's dog, black and white.

"I," said the dove from the rafters high,
"I cooed him to sleep so he would not cry.
We cooed him to sleep, my mate and I.
I," said the dove from the rafters high.

Thus every beast by some good spell,
in the stable dark was glad to tell,
of the gift he gave Emmanuel,
the gift he gave Emmanuel.